THE PICTURE STORYBOOK

By Cathy West • Illustrated by Diane de Groat

Piper Books

First published in the USA 1988 by Random House, Inc., NY
and simultaneously by Random House of Canada Limited, Toronto.
This Piper edition published in Great Britain and simultaneousiy in
Eire by Pan Books Ltd, Cavaye Place, London SW10 9PG
9 8 7 6 5 4 3 2 1
Copyright © 1988 Lucasfilm Ltd. (LFL). All rights reserved
under International and Pan-American Copyright Conventions.
TM & © 1988 Lucasfilm Ltd. (LFL). All rights reserved.
Pan Books Ltd., authorized user.
ISBN 0 330 3062 4
Printed and bound in Great Britain by Springbourne Press Ltd., Basildon.

Long ago, high in a stone castle, there lived a wicked queen named Bavmorda, who ruled all the land with her evil magic.

Then one day, in the queen's dark dungeon, a baby was born. In most ways she was like any other baby. But on her arm was a special mark. An ancient prophecy foretold that this tiny baby girl would grow up to be a good and wise queen. Only she could end Queen Bavmorda's evil rule.

But Bavmorda knew of this and planned to kill the baby! To save her, a kind servant smuggled the baby out of the castle and set her afloat down the river in a tiny raft. She hoped someone would find the baby and take care of her.

Downstream was a land of hardworking little people called Nelwyns. Two children were playing tag by the river while their father, Willow Ufgood, plowed his fields nearby. Suddenly the little girl spotted something through the reeds.

"Daddy! Daddy!" she cried. "Come look—it's a baby!"

Willow ran to the river. "It must be a Daikini," he said. "See how big it is? Daikinis are giants who live far away."

"Let's keep her!" the children shouted.

But Willow was not so sure. "We must keep her a secret till we decide what to do," he said.

The next day was a Nelwyn holiday. Willow had waited all year to put on a magic show, for he longed to be a magician more than anything in the world.

In one trick he made a pig disappear! But then the pig squealed and jumped out of the secret pocket in Willow's cape. Everyone laughed when they saw it was not real magic.

Suddenly a Death Dog from Queen Bavmorda's castle ran through the festival! It tore up wagons and huts, then ran away.

A frightened woman held up the pieces of a broken cradle. "It was looking for someone's baby!" she cried.

Willow knew he could no longer keep the Daikini baby a secret.

A town meeting was called. Willow brought the baby before the High Aldwin, the village wise man, and told how he had found her.

"I sense that this baby is special," said the High Aldwin. "But we are in danger as long as she is here. You must return her to the land of the Daikinis."

Such a trip would be very dangerous, but Willow agreed to go.

Willow had never traveled beyond his own village, but the next day he bravely set off into the forest. It was a long, hard journey.

On the way he met a warrior named Madmartigan.

"Can you help me?" asked Willow. "I must return this baby to her people."

"I'm on my way to teach Bavmorda's army a lesson," said Madmartigan. "But we'll meet again, my little friend. And then I promise to help you *and* the baby."

So Willow struggled on alone. In a magical forest he was captured by two tiny brownies named Rool and Franjean, who introduced him to Cherlindrea, the beautiful queen of the fairies.

"This baby is very special," said Cherlindrea, "for she will grow up to be queen of all the world. She has chosen you, Willow Ufgood, to take her to the castle of Tir Asleen, where a good king will take care of her until she is old enough to rule."

"She doesn't want me!" cried Willow. "She needs a strong soldier or a powerful magician to take her on a trip like that!"

Cherlindrea just smiled and said, "Here is my magic wand. Take it to a good sorceress named Raziel, and she will help you."

Willow and the brownies journeyed through the forest. Along the way they met Madmartigan again.

"Queen Bavmorda's soldiers are everywhere," he said. "It's not safe for you to travel alone with the baby." Then he grinned. "Lucky for you you've got the best soldier in the world to protect you—me!" Laughing, he led them on their way.

Soon Franjean pointed in the distance at a mystical island. "There," he said. "That's where you'll find Raziel."

The sky grew dark with thunderclouds. Willow left the baby on the shore with Madmartigan and the brownies, then rowed alone across the storm-tossed waters.

When Willow reached the island, he met a furry little possum. "I'm looking for Raziel the sorceress," he said.

"I am Raziel!" said the possum. "Queen Bavmorda cast a spell on me. The island is cursed too. We must leave right away!"

Quickly they rowed back across the water. But when they reached the shore, they were captured by the evil General Kael, leader of Queen Bavmorda's soldiers. The soldiers brought Willow and his friends to their camp, high in the snow-covered mountains.

Late that night, in their dark prison cage, Raziel tried to teach Willow some quick magic. He held the wand and spoke the magic words that would transform Raziel and help them escape.

The wand began to wiggle. Sparks flew!

"Try harder, Willow!" cried Raziel. Then her voice began to squawk. Her brown fur turned into black feathers.

Willow had changed her into a bird!

"Oh, no," moaned Willow as he dropped the smoking wand. "How will we ever get out of here now?"

"Let us try!" cried the brownies. And they used their tiny spears to break open the lock.

Willow and his friends hurried into the dark night. Soon they found the tent where the baby was being held prisoner. Willow slipped inside and tiptoed past the sleeping guard.

But the guard heard him and woke up.

"The prisoners are escaping!" shouted the guard.

Outside, Madmartigan began fighting the soldiers! In all the confusion Willow spotted a soldier's shield sliding across the snow.

Willow held the baby tight as he and Madmartigan jumped on. With a *whoosh!* they scooted down the mountainside in the wildest sled ride ever, leaving the queen's soldiers far behind.

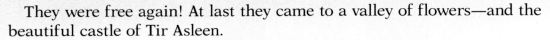

They were free again! At last they came to a valley of flowers—and the beautiful castle of Tir Asleen.

"Hurray! We're safe!" cried Willow.

"Don't be so sure," replied Madmartigan.

Inside, the people could not shout their greetings—for they stood frozen inside statues made of crystal.

"Queen Bavmorda must have cast a spell over the castle!" squawked Raziel. "Hurry, Willow. You must try again to change me."

Willow twirled the magic wand. He was right in the middle of a magic chant when the sound of horses made him turn his head.

"Willow! Pay attention!" cried Raziel. But it was too late! Raziel changed into a goat as Bavmorda's soldiers arrived with evil General Kael leading the charge.

Madmartigan bravely fought the soldiers, but there were far too many of them. They surrounded Willow, and General Kael grabbed the baby from his arms. Then the soldiers galloped off toward Queen Bavmorda's castle.

"Don't worry," Madmartigan told Willow. "We'll save her. Come on!" And Willow and his friends hurried after them.

Finally they reached Queen Bavmorda's castle. High in a dark tower they heard the baby cry.

"Willow, use the wand," said Raziel. "And be careful this time!"

Willow held the wand steady. He closed his eyes tight and thought only of the magic. Carefully he spoke the strange words Raziel had taught him: "*Danalor...danu, danu, luatha danu...*"

The powerful wand began to shake. And then—it worked!

Now they could enter the castle.

Willow and Raziel sneaked into the castle. At the top of the queen's tower, Raziel waved her wand—and the heavy door swung open.

"You cannot have the baby!" Queen Bavmorda cried wildly. "I must destroy her to break the prophecy!"

Raziel charged into the room. The air crackled as she used her good magic to fight the evil magic of the queen. But finally Bavmorda seized Raziel's wand and cast a spell that sent her into a deep sleep.

Then Queen Bavmorda turned to Willow and the baby. "You cannot escape!" she cried. "I will draw lightning from the sky and send this child into eternal darkness!"

"No!" shouted Willow. "I am a great magician! And I say you cannot have her!" He swirled his cape around himself.

And the baby disappeared!

"How did you do that?" screamed Bavmorda. In a fit of anger, she shook the wand at the sky. Lightning flashed! It struck the tip of the wand.

The evil queen exploded in a magical burst of fireworks—and disappeared forever.

Suddenly Madmartigan burst into the room. "I have done away with General Kael. Where is the baby?"

Willow pulled the baby from the secret pocket of his cape. "She's safe!" he said. "I fooled the queen with my disappearing pig trick. It worked a lot better than when I tried it at the Nelwyn fair!"

Now that the baby was safe, Willow was eager to return home. He had a lot to tell. For he had finally realized his dream. He was a real magician now! And he had saved the baby. The prophecy would now come true!